CAUGHT LOOKING BY THE BASKETEER

Straight to Gay First Time Story

Michael Levi

ISBN: 9798414903321
Imprint: Independently published

1st edition

Cover design by: Michael Levi

CONTENTS

CHAPTER 1

He pushed his shoulder against me, opening a big and bright smile on his face. "Dude, you're not going to win against me this time," Carl said and I returned my attention to the game. It didn't matter how good he thought he was, he wasn't going to win against me. Not again and not this time.

Or at least, that was what I was trying to convince myself about.

His car was hundreds of feet in front of mine, jumping over a small hill as he kicked up dust behind it. I pressed the button harder and even leaned in slightly on the couch, but I couldn't catch up to him.

Sweat was pooling on my forehead even though the heating system in the unit was barely keeping up with the cold coming from the outside. I took a glance through the window and couldn't help but think that it looked so pretty. I wanted to go there and play in the snow, but Carl didn't and I didn't have anyone else to play with.

I focused back on the race, erasing my previous thoughts before pressing the button so much harder this time I thought it would never return to normal. I was closing the distance between him and me – or was I? – and I was feeling excited about it.

My heart was pounding in my chest. My eyes were so focused on the race that I couldn't even blink. If someone were to put his hand on my shoulder, I'd jump off the couch and fall face-first on the floor. That's how focused I was on winning this game.

I was a very competitive guy and I wasn't hiding that.

I turned the stick to the left when a curve was nearing as something caught the attention of my eyes, coming from the corner of my eyes. Those giggles… I could have heard them anywhere and I'd still have recognized them. They came from my crush. She usually shared the same classes with me and was strolling outside with her friends.

I heard something crashing, the sound of metal bending and glass shattering. I snapped my head back to the television as I realized that it was my car which had just veered off the dirt path and was now flipping over the terrain, eventually crashing against one of the trees.

Carl looked at me with a dirty smile on his face. It was the smile of someone who knew he'd won. He was also very competitive and didn't like losing, no matter who his opponent was.

"Dude, I just knew you were going to lose. You have such a huge crush on her," he said, seconds later speeding through the finish line as the race ended. I slumped on the couch, letting the control fall out of my hand and onto the carpet.

I turned my head to look through the window again and couldn't see my crush anymore. I couldn't even hear her voice, which was just as disappointing. I liked hearing her voice. There was just something about it I couldn't put my finger on.

"I know…" I said, not feeling confident in myself and willing to have another race with him.

He nudged my shoulder again, making me feel the hardness of his muscles. Carl was a basketball player. A basketeer, as they liked to call it, and he was always training and playing sports games. Even now I could see a pile of NBA games next to the TV and the console, and they were from different years and versions. He didn't play any game that wasn't basketball, unless he was playing against me, in which case he always went along with my choices.

I should've chosen something that I could win more easily

against him.

"Bro, there's no point overthinking it. You gotta approach her and show her how you really feel about it. Chicks like her fall hard for nerdy guys like you."

I gave him a weak smile. I didn't know what he was talking about, but it wasn't helping things. Carl was a good guy, even if he was misguided sometimes. He also had his fair share of chicks that thought they liked him, but in the end, they always dumped him.

That was why he was stuck with me now. Well, one of the other important reasons behind that was that it was snowing like hell outside, too. We could still be doing something outside if we wanted to.

The truth was that Carl was such a good friend of mine that he preferred doing whatever I was doing.

I wished I was more like him. I wished I had his height, his confidence when picking up girls, and that stubble on his face that really made him look older than the 18-year-old self that he was.

He picked up my controller with just one hand and shoved it back into my hands. "C'mon, dude. There's no point feeling so down about it. Let's go for another race and make it a little more appetizing this time. How about betting on something with me?"

"You mean… like a dare?" I asked, analyzing his face and realizing there was something else about it I admired – his teeth. They were professionally white, perfectly shaped, and I couldn't see anything wrong with them. No wonder that different classmates, men and women alike, fell in love with him easily.

His face was always so captivating and with a smile like that, he could make anyone think that he was the most welcoming and trustworthy guy in the world. That's what I thought of him and it was one of the reasons why I also thought that living with him was going to be a breeze. I'd thought that living with another guy was going to bring different complications to my life, but that wasn't what was happening.

I pushed some buttons on the controller and we were soon

choosing a race track and our cars. I picked the same car from before, eager to show him that I was going to win this time.

I looked at his face again as I asked, "So, what are we betting on?"

He looked at me, pulling up his eyebrow.

"Bro, I don't think you want to know."

I perked up, feeling more curious about it. When he mentioned the dare, I didn't give it much thought, but now that he said that, he got my attention. I was dying to find out what he wanted to do in case I lost.

I brushed my elbow against his shoulder.

"Dude, don't leave me hanging here. Whatever you're thinking we should bet on, tell me. I'm not going to give up until you spill everything out."

Carl brushed his fingers through his hair. He had short, blond hair, and even though I was pretty sure he didn't do anything special with it, it looked pretty smooth and shiny against the light coming through the windows.

"Are you sure about that, Ashton, you dirty Aussie?" He asked, mentioning the fact that I was Australian and blond as well. But even though we had similar physical attributes, we weren't very similar. He was tall, strong, confident, and also had perfect vision. He didn't have to wear glasses as I did.

I analyzed his face again. Blinking twice, I said, "Now that you brought up the dare, spill it out. Leaving me hanging like this is torture."

He shook his head. "Alright, Jesus. Don't worry. Since you are so curious about it, then I'm going to tell you what it is."

Seconds later, he was just looking at me and I couldn't help but wonder if he was pulling my leg.

I nudged his shoulder with my elbow again and we burst out laughing. There was nothing quite like bonding with my bro and we were quickly becoming very good friends, I could tell.

When he stopped laughing, he shoved his hand against my

thigh, grabbing it. It wasn't that I was insecure about my sexual orientation, but I never thought that his hand was so big and heavy. We never touched each other before this.

I felt something weird coming up in my body, making my heart warmer. I looked at his face and eyes, wondering what was going on in his head. We weren't gay unless we were going further than this, right? I shook that thought out of my mind as I realized it was stupid.

He leaned in closer to me as he said, "Dude, there's just no way you're bigger than me."

I blinked twice, not understanding what he was talking about. "What are you going on about?" I asked, pushing him away from me because he was so close I could smell the aroma coming out of his mouth. It was pretty minty and clean. Carl was the kind of guy who brushed his teeth often.

"There was this one day you were boasting to your friends that you are bigger than me. I heard it when you were in your room."

I really had no idea what he was talking about and it was puzzling me.

CHAPTER 2

Blinking again, I was hoping that whatever he was talking about was going to be cleared up in the next few seconds. I was beginning to think I could remember when that happened, but this all still felt so forced. It was almost like Carl had been thinking about bringing up this subject for a long time.

"Bigger than you in what sense?" I asked, forgetting about the game we were playing.

He gave me a knowing look.

"Dude, you know what I'm talking about."

I scrunched up my eyebrows, but I didn't do so because I was confused. I did it because I never thought that this subject would ever be brought up between us.

"I don't think I ever talked about that. Come on, bro. You know how gay that is."

"It still doesn't explain what I heard."

"You must've been drunk at the time. That's the only logical explanation I can think of right now."

"I sure as hell wasn't."

After saying that, he held his hand out in front of me. I looked at it, not understanding what was going on anymore.

"This must be some kind of joke," I said, almost wishing I could pinch myself and wake up from whatever was going on. This was making me feel very uncomfortable, which was something I thought would never happen when I was with Carl. He was such a good friend that I was already feeling much better than all the times I was with my high school buddies.

"You said you were going to bet on it with me, and I don't want to see you chickening out on it. Come on, dude. I'm not letting you escape from this."

I glanced at his hand and then at his face, seeing that his smile was telling me just one thing – that it didn't matter what I thought of it. If I didn't bet on it with him, he would make my life a living hell. Carl was the kind of guy who didn't drop something he was obsessed with until he got what he wanted.

I took a deep breath in and shook his hand. I was still nervous about it, but it was better than letting him think that I was a coward. I really wasn't and if he wanted so much to find out who was bigger, then I was willing to go through with it.

"Alright, then. Whoever loses the next race will have to show his cock."

I gulped, tipping up my glasses. Just like with everything about us, I was pretty sure that we were going to find out he was actually bigger than me. I didn't want to think about it this way, but the way he was so obsessed with it meant that he felt pretty confident about the size of his cock.

I was still dazzled by all the things happening here, though. Were we really going to do it? Was I really going to have to lower my shorts and show him my dick? For some reason, thinking that it might actually happen was making me feel excited and scared about it. There was just something raw and natural about the whole thing, and I didn't know if that was supposed to make me feel more scared.

"Ready or not, we're doing this," he affirmed, raising his voice and sounding more confident in his skills all of a sudden. I supposed that was so because it didn't matter if he thought he was going to lose. Even if he did, he'd still come out of this on top. After all, being bigger than me had its positives and one of them was knowing that he could never lose against me when it came to that.

Sweat pooling on Carl's forehead, he was so focused on what he was doing that he was leaning into the TV. My hands were shaking. The race had started and we were toe to toe. There was something about me I never told him, and it was that I was pretty good at learning the ins and outs of a race track after getting to know what it was like.

That was why I was doing much better now than before.

The end of the race was in sight and I was almost prevailing, though only by a difference of a couple of milliseconds. Carl glanced to the right, brushing his leg against me and making me feel the hair on it. I didn't want to think about it that way, but I realized that what he did meant a lot more than what met the eye.

Carl was trying to cheat and I knew it.

My thumb pushed the vehicle to the right when I wanted to make it go to the left, and I cursed it. I mumbled something along the lines of 'cheating motherfucker' through my breath when I noticed that now he was a couple of milliseconds in front of me, and it was useless thinking that I could make up the difference.

Seconds later, his car as muddy as mine, hopped over the small hill before the finishing line and he triumphed. I was left flabbergasted, already weighing the outcomes of what losing to him meant. I was going to have to lower my shorts for Carl, which was something I thought I'd never have to do.

He put his controller down on the carpet, sinking his hand onto my thigh again. This time, he did something I thought he'd never do. After all, he'd been with plenty of chicks and dated so many of them that I'd lost count. I didn't need to have lived with him for long to know that. His Instagram account showed me as much.

Carl was kneading the skin of my thigh with his hand, and I didn't know how to feel about that. After all, if I ever did something like that with him, the first thing he'd do is yell that I was being gay.

But finally, he drove his hand away, even though I had to be honest and say that I was liking it. He made me feel… slightly safer and that we really were building a strong bond between us? Even trying to make sense of my feelings was difficult and so I didn't keep trying.

"Dude, this is so gay," I said, wishing that I could rewind time and pretend that nothing of this was happening.

"Not more gay than you chickening out on it," he said, his eyes going up and down like he was checking me out.

I stood up right away, my hands trembling slightly. I knew what was going to happen, and I didn't like it. I was going to show him my dick, he was going to laugh out loud at it, and then I'd forever live with the shame of knowing that I was much smaller than my roommate. Next term and I'd already have to start thinking about moving out…

"No way I'm going to do this," I said, sounding determined – or at least as determined as I thought I sounded. I was pretty sure that a blond guy with glasses and blue eyes didn't look very convincing when he was trying to look tough, especially when he didn't have much in terms of muscles. I wasn't skinny, but a guy like Carl would still wipe the floor with me and it didn't help things that he was like a head taller than me.

That all became more evident when he slowly stood up and walked over to me, smiling as he did so.

"C'mon, dude. Don't disappoint me like that."

"You're really going to do this? With your roommate? What will you think of me from then on? I'll cease being just your roommate."

"And you think this never happened to me before? C'mon, this isn't the first time that I'm seeing another guy's dick," he joked, picking up something from the bookshelf. It was a ruler. I didn't think that we really were doing this. I thought that he was just joking.

Carl stopped in front of me, cocking up his eyebrows like he was daring me to keep saying 'no'. I could tell what he'd say if that happened. He'd tell everyone in college that I was a pussy and he wouldn't be ashamed to tell them what the dare was about, too.

I gulped, putting my fingers under the band of my shorts. If I couldn't win against it, then I had to pretend that this wasn't turning me on. And it wasn't, really. The only thing that it was making me feel was more… uncomfortable around him, which was nothing different than everything that had been going on between us for a pretty long time. Since first meeting him, to be more precise.

Gulping again, I lowered my shorts and reaffirmed that I couldn't back out.

CHAPTER 3

He widened his eyes slightly as he looked down at my cock. I didn't know what was in his eyes, but I could tell that he was showing some slight interest in what he was seeing. He still had the ruler in his hand and I could tell that he wasn't thinking about dropping what was happening anytime soon.

My shorts and my pair of briefs were on my knees, and my dick was out and bouncing up and down. I bit my bottom lip, not because I was horny, but because I was so nervous that my hands were getting sweatier.

"Dude, this is so gay," I said again, wishing that things were different. I was cursing the fact that I had to play that multiplayer game with him, but now that I was thinking about it, I wanted to make it so I could go back to it.

"You keep saying that, but you aren't going to change my mind about it," he said, getting on one knee in front of me. He was going to use the ruler to measure the size of my dick.

I stepped away from him, putting my hand out in front of him.

Carl looked up. "What's going on?" He asked, making me realize that he was really confused about what I was doing. "I thought you weren't a chicken."

I lowered my hand as I tried to recompose myself. "I'm not. It's just that I'm trying to..."

He scrunched up his eyebrows as he shot his hand for my waist and grabbed me, yanking me to him. I almost fell over as I realized his hand was so close to my ass he could almost feel the skin.

My dick was semi-hard and I didn't know what I was feeling anymore. I shouldn't be feeling turned on by what was happening. After all, it didn't matter how gay the things we were doing were. I was still as straight as an arrow.

"What the hell are you doing?" I asked, feeling more shocked than ever before.

"Dude, this isn't anything new for me, like I said."

He looked at me like he was unsurprised by my reaction. I couldn't help but wonder what happened before where he was put in a similar situation.

Moments later, he said, "Make it hard so that I can measure it, unless you want to think you are even smaller than I think you are."

The thought that I was going to have to pump my dick right in front of my roommate was weird and a turn-on at the same time. My hand was shaking, but I still moved to where my cock was and I enclosed my fingers around it.

"You are uncut, just like me," he pointed out, making me widen my eyes in genuine surprise. I never thought he was going to bring up such a detail.

"You are making this look more gay than it is. I sure as hell hope you are feeling completely comfortable about everything you are doing. Otherwise, you will never be able to fall asleep again."

Carl smirked. "Bro, don't worry about it. As long as you keep your lips shut about this, I won't tell anyone."

I examined his eyes as I realized he was indeed telling the truth. As long as I didn't tell anyone about this, nobody would find out, which was very comforting.

Before he could measure my dick with the ruler, I asked, "And how big are you?"

He looked up, curling up the corner of his lips. "Do you really want to find out? Just looking at your dick right now, I can tell that you are pretty small."

"Dude, fuck you. Just get on with this already." That's what I said, trying to sound tougher than I was, even though I was feeling anything but.

"You are so impatient you look cute," he said and it came out of his mouth like it didn't matter to him. He just called me 'cute', which was something I thought I'd never hear coming from him.

He put the ruler next to my cock and it gave a little twitch. I didn't know why it happened, or perhaps I knew why it did and I just didn't want to admit it. Even though it was a little cold inside, my body was warmer and I was sweating a little. I didn't know if Carl had already noticed it, and I sure as hell was hoping I was going to get through this without that happening.

For a moment, he couldn't stop looking at my cock and I was wondering why that was. It was like he was mesmerized by it, which couldn't be further from the truth. After all, he was also straight like an arrow and he had dated so many women in his life he couldn't even be bisexual. He never showed any interest in men. None that I knew of, anyway.

After he finished lining up the ruler to my cock, his eyes moved left and right as he read the numbers. When he moved the ruler away, I couldn't help but feel impatient about what the reading was. After all, it was one thing measuring the size of one's dick and another having someone else doing it for me.

He stood up, put the ruler on the couch, and looked at me with a mocking smile on his face.

Now that he had finished measuring the size of my shaft, I attempted to put my shorts back on as he waggled his finger in front of him.

"No, no, no, bro. I don't think you're going to do that."

"Why not? You already did what you had to do. I want to stop this madness before it makes me feel gay."

"I think it's only fair that I showed you how big I am, too," he said, widening his dirty smile. The longer this was going on, the more it was making me feel afraid of what might happen. I never thought that the beginning of my life with him was going to lead to this.

But it wasn't like I was completely objecting to it, too. In fact, part of my body was welcoming it.

I didn't want to admit it, but I was a little turned on by the fact that I was half-naked in front of this huge guy.

"Now that's gay."

"No homo." And after a moment of silence, Carl added, "So, what is it going to be? Do you want me to show it to you or not?"

I grabbed my shorts as I was beginning to think that things were getting out of control. I mean, it was one thing making sure that I wasn't backing out on the dare and another going on with this.

He narrowed his eyes as he made sure I wasn't going to do that, and I didn't. It wasn't worth going against someone so much stronger, who was clearly the alpha in our house.

I gulped. There was no denying that part of my mind wanted him to do that, even though I had to keep saying to myself that I wasn't gay. Really, I wasn't. This was the first time I was doing anything like this with another guy.

"Let's bet on it again," I proposed, studying his eyes to see what his reaction was going to be. I thought he was going to take it well and thus I wasn't surprised when his expression softened up. "Let's play another race."

"But I'm not letting you put your shorts back on."

I widened my eyes, my heart feeling tight. "Why not? Do you want me to win the race against you half-naked?"

He cackled. "I promise I won't tell anyone about it, bro."

I looked at the couch, spotting the controller. The thought that I was going to have to play another race, only that this time I was going to be half-naked made me feel a little uncomfortable, but also excited. There was always going to be something exciting about doing anything new for the first time.

He grabbed his controller and held it in front of him as he teased me.

"So, Ashton, what is it going to be? Do you want to potentially see that you are not as small as you think you are?"

He rubbed his crotch, making me look down at it. It wouldn't be a problem if I just glanced down, but the fact was that I held my gaze and I didn't realize I was doing that until it was too late. When I looked back up, Carl was already widening his smirk.

"Something caught your attention, bro?" He asked, sitting back down on the couch.

I sighed and went back to the couch without pulling up my shorts. I knew that I was possibly making a mistake, but I was going on with it.

CHAPTER 4

Sweat was soaking my armpits as the race went on. I thought I was going to win it. This time, I was way more prepared for whatever distractions might pop up. I wasn't going to divert my attention from the screen to anything happening on the outside, no matter who was there. Even if my crush was walking outside the house, I was going to keep my attention focused on the TV.

My dick was a little softer right now, but it was still hard. I had no idea if Carl had noticed that, but he hadn't, so far, said anything about it. His attention was also focused on the TV. He said that, if he won the race, he'd show me his cock and I was kind of excited about it.

I mean, he saw my shaft and he said that it didn't look impressive. If anything, he made me feel inferior to him – more so than I already did. I needed to get one up on him, no matter the cost. That was why I was going to win the race no matter what. I was going to make it so he didn't lower his shorts in front of me.

He could lower his shorts in front of anyone else he wanted. Why was he even so obsessed with me right now?

The car veered to the right, speeding up as much as it could. He was right behind me, his car kicking up dirt and dust. It was a very exciting race and one of the most exciting I had played in this game.

The finishing line was a couple of feet ahead and I was pretty sure that I was going to win. I even looked to the left as our eyes met again and I saw the confirmation I was looking for. His lips were slightly trembling and I could tell that this wasn't the outcome he was looking for.

I focused my attention back on the screen as I realized it wasn't what I was looking for, either. I didn't know if this was my mind playing tricks on me, but I wanted to know everything about my roommate. I would be one of the few people in the world who knew about the size of his dick.

I gulped, pressing the other button as I slowed the car down. I knew that I was possibly making a mistake, but this time, I was taking matters into my own hands. If he was going to show me his cock one way or the other, then it was better that he did it because of a decision of mine.

His car blasted through the finishing line as the race finally ended.

Carl shot up from the couch, his eyes wide in surprise. He dropped the controller as he threw his hands over his head, fisting them.

"Bro, I thought I was going to lose for sure this time!"

I stood up, putting the controller back on the couch as I shrugged.

"What can I say? You are just so much better than me in the game, dude."

He waggled his eyebrows as he put his fingers under the bands of his shorts.

"So, I guess this really is happening, Ashton," he said, slowly lowering his shorts as I found out that I couldn't take my eyes off of his crotch. Goddammit, now he really was going to think that I was gay and there would be nothing about that I'd be able to do. I was feeling a little desperate, but also a little turned on. My hard dick was telling me as much right now.

He finished lowering his shorts and I could finally see the size of his bulge. Good lord. I knew that he was big, but I didn't think I was going to be looking at that. It was like I was looking at something that didn't belong to him. It was protruding from between his legs, almost like it was teasing me.

And to make matters worse, he grabbed his bulge and gave it a little pull, as if he was daring me to get closer. But I didn't do that. I didn't want to admit to Carl what was going on in my mind. The less he knew that I found him incredibly big, the better.

"Time for the final act, dude," he mocked, lowering his underwear as his dick came out. First, it was the head and then the rest of it, bouncing up and down, and he was already hard from the get-go. Now that I was thinking about it, that time when he mentioned he did this kind of thing with other guys… Could it mean that he was… gay? I didn't think so, I reaffirmed to myself, but the longer this was going on, the more I was thinking that something was up.

We were just bros, right?

And, holy shit. I knew that he was bigger than me, but I didn't think that he was that thick, heavy, and long. He could wreck me sideways with that thing and I was pretty sure that I wouldn't be able to walk after that, too. That was why I couldn't stop looking at it. Carl was also uncut and his head was pretty and attention-drawing. I couldn't momentarily move my eyes away from it and that was saying something considering that, every time I watched porn, I never focused on the men.

He looped his fingers around his massive dong, giving it a couple of strokes. "So, what do you think, bro? It's pretty big, isn't it?"

"Dude, fuck you. I thought you were just joking." I was breathless, feeling like I'd just finished running the longest marathon in the world.

He widened his smile, approaching me. I stepped away, not admitting the fact that I was hard and couldn't do anything about it. Worse, I could feel saliva building up on the back of my mouth.

"Wanna measure it? To make sure that it really is that big?"

I studied his eyes, finding that unbelievable. It was one thing him showing me his dick like this and another him asking me to measure it. I mean, I was aware that he did the same thing for me, but I thought that by now he'd have dropped the matter and directed his attention toward something else.

"Fuck you, man. I'm not getting close to that thing."

"Yes, you are. You're already closer to it than most people will ever be."

I looked at his eyes, finding out that they were showing his determination. He wanted to go through with this and there was nothing that I could do. I mean, I could keep objecting to it, but then he'd keep bullying me about it and I was pretty sure I wouldn't last very long…

He picked up the ruler, shoving it to my face.

"C'mon, dude. Let's do this one more thing." He gave his dick a couple more strokes, teasing me to go on with it. "Let's measure it and put it to rest. I promise you that you won't even have to touch it."

I gulped. "I won't?"

The fact that he was saying that was making me think there was something about it he wasn't telling me, like a plan that he was planning on setting in motion as soon as I was near his dick.

And I meant nearer than I was right now… I was so close that I could smell it. It was that characteristic smell of sweat, his perfume, and pee. It was going through my nostrils and impregnating my lungs.

"Pinky promise," he said, holding out his hand and showing me his pinky. I looked at it, pondering what he said. I didn't think that Carl was lying, but still… he wasn't exactly the most trustworthy of people in the world. I still remembered what his other 'bros' had said to me before when I asked them some questions about him, and I would never forget what they said.

He gave his dick a couple more strokes, his balls looking heavy. They hung low, which was an interesting contrast to my tight and small balls. Perhaps that was telling me something else about him – that he hadn't cummed in a pretty long time and was looking forward to doing that now. Nevertheless, I wasn't and I was keeping that in mind.

Or was I? Now that we had gone through so much together in so little time, I couldn't help but wonder if he was more potent than I was. I wondered if his milk was whiter, thicker, and less transparent. Those were just curious questions popping up in my mind right now, though, and I wasn't going to act on them.

"Come on, bro. I'm already feeling impatient."

CHAPTER 5

My hand was shaking, but I still picked up at the ruler and went down on my knees. If I thought that his cock was impressive before, now it was something completely different. I was level with it. It was right in front of my eyes and I couldn't even blink.

I didn't want to admit it, but–

"Do you want to suck it, bro?" He breathed, making me shoot my eyes up. I never thought that he was going to ask that question and much less make it sound so normal.

My lips were trembling, but I still mustered up enough strength to say, "Of course not, man. I'm not gay."

He cackled. "The way you are looking at it, you could have mistaken me. You could've made me think of something else."

I shook my head and put the ruler where it was supposed to be, from the base of his cock to the head. My eyes went wide when I realized it was almost as long as the ruler.

"I'm just going to get on with this before it's too late and before I make a mistake."

And meanwhile, I couldn't help but feel the warmth coming from his body. I knew that he was hot, but I didn't think he was this hot. An alien thought was beginning to show up in my mind. I was beginning to wonder what it would be like if I grabbed his cock like he was proposing. He said that I could suck him off if I wanted to, but I was pretty sure that it involved a lot more than that.

"It's really big." I looked up and I thought I was going to see his eyes mocking me, but I was witnessing the opposite. He was looking at me with lust in them.

I didn't want to admit it, but Carl had a crush on me.

I put the ruler back on the couch slowly and when I tried to stand up, he put his hand on my shoulder. I couldn't move. I mean, if I tried to scoot away from him as quickly as I could, I was pretty sure I would be able to, but I was choosing not to do that. And the reason behind that was pretty simple. I didn't want to disappoint myself.

After all, I was beginning to grow more and more curious about what it would be like if I sucked him off.

"You promise you won't tell anyone about this?" I asked, my heart speeding up.

He nodded, giving me some comfort.

"Don't worry about it. My lips are sealed, bro."

I looked down at his cock, realizing that my curiosity was getting the better of me. This was my only chance to suck another guy off.

He gave his dick a couple more strokes, making it look really hard. It was pointing right to my mouth and it was very bulbous, pre-come coming out through the slit.

"I thought you weren't gay," I pointed out.

"What are you talking about? I'm not. We are just experimenting."

"Then why are you so turned on?" I asked. "I can see the pre-come coming out."

"It's just for lubrication, man. It will make it easy for you to suck me."

I gulped, realizing that there was no turning back. It was more than curiosity that was driving me toward doing this. I was doing it because I knew it was going to be good.

He didn't shave before and I was beginning to wonder what it was going to be like to feel my face pressing against his pubes. His cockhead was just so red, almost like all of his blood was there.

"Don't keep me waiting," he advised and I decided to take things slow.

My hand was trembling as I put my fingers around his shaft, realizing that my thumb just barely touched my other fingers.

"Jesus fuck, man. It's too big. You are so fucking lucky."

"Quit complimenting me and just suck me off already," he groaned, putting his hand on the back of my head as he brought it down. I had just about enough time to open my mouth before I felt his shaft going right in, breaching through every possible barrier.

I thought that I was opening my mouth wide enough for it, but it was a little more complicated than that. I felt his cockhead brushing against the top of my mouth and my gag reflexes started to kick in, but I held them back. I wasn't going to let them ruin the moment I was having with my roommate.

My roommate… Thinking about it, I couldn't help but admit that our friendship was going to be much different from now on.

And when his dick was inside my mouth and I could feel it pressing against the back of my throat, I couldn't help but feel that I was in heaven. For a moment, I could forget about all the problems going on in my life.

I didn't have much experience with what I was doing, but I was using my tongue however I could to swirl it around his dickhead. I kept doing that for what felt like an eternity until I decided to start going up and down along it, feeling the entirety of his length.

And the most interesting about it was that I was beginning to get used to it, all the while saying that I really wasn't gay.

He brushed his hand over my head and I liked that he was doing that. It was like he was complimenting me for my cocksucking skills, which was something I never thought would happen.

"Dude, who taught you that? You're better at this than most of my girlfriends were."

I just groaned, my head bouncing up and down along his cock.

I didn't have time to answer him. I was way more preoccupied with giving him a good head, and I could tell that he was enjoying it.

He brushed his fingers through my hair, grabbed a handful of them, and then started to dictate the pace he wanted. I kept circling my tongue around his beautiful cock, tasting his pre-come. It was slightly salty, which was a prelude to what I knew was awaiting me.

I could feel that his cock was beginning to throb and I was excited about it. He was going to come inside my mouth and I couldn't wait to feel what that was going to be like.

I grabbed his thighs as I waited for the inevitable. I was happily going up and down along his cock with a smile on my face, but then he pulled my head up and away from his shaft.

Seeing what was happening, I couldn't help but look up and wonder what was going on in his mind. I thought that he was going to let me keep sucking him off. I thought that he was enjoying it.

"What happened?" I asked, my voice sounding weaker than normal.

"I just thought that you should finally admit it."

"Admit what?"

"That you are gay. A straight dude would never be so happy sucking another guy off. You were going to make me come inside your mouth and you weren't even trying to stop me."

I gulped, feeling that my throat was drier than normal. I was so happy and nervous at the same time. I never thought that I was going to be doing this with my roommate and getting so intimate with him.

"I guess there's no point in hiding the truth anymore. I am gay, at least for you."

He smiled without showing his teeth. "Great. I knew you were going to say that. That means you can join up with a little friend of ours. He's very much like you. Justin turned him not too long ago."

"Turned him? What are you talking about?"

He waved his hand. "Don't worry about it. I'll introduce you to him when the time is right."

I gulped as I realized that all the masks were down and now we were beginning a different friendship - one with plenty of benefits.

After a moment of silence, as I was beginning to wonder what else was on his mind, he said, "Get on all fours, dude. I'm going to bring the lube."

"Lube?" I croaked even though I knew what he was talking about. He was going to penetrate me with that cock of his. If my mind was still thinking there was a way to tell myself I wasn't gay, then doing so now was pointless. It was beyond my control.

"The lube, yeah. There's only one way we are finishing this."

I gulped, but I knew I had to do what he wanted. I turned around slowly, got on all fours, and opened my asshole as wide as I could for him. He went to his bedroom and then came back with a bottle of lube in his hand. He screwed it open, spread some of the substance on his hand, and then knelt behind me.

He touched his finger to my asshole, drawing small circles on it as he followed the path filled with small ridges and hills. Shivers ran down my spine as I started to moan and groan. I never thought that having another man brushing his finger along my asshole was going to feel so good.

It was like Carl had done this plenty of times before, and given what he said a couple of minutes ago, I was pretty sure that was the case.

Then, he penetrated me with one of his fingers. It went right in without any difficulty. Seconds later, he started to rub his finger inside my rectum. I closed my eyes and focused only on what he was making me feel. My dick was hard – so much so that I was already climaxing.

After it stopped throbbing, he slapped my ass as he said, "I didn't think you were feeling so good about this. Maybe we should do this again another time. What do you think about making this something a bit more permanent?"

"I think that would be great," I breathed, just waiting for him to penetrate me with his big shaft.

When he was done lubing up my rectum and he was satisfied with my ring, he put the bottle of lube on the floor and grabbed my waist before pulling me to him. I felt his crimson cockhead nudging my orifice, which was the prelude to what he was going to do.

He cocked his head before he said, "Last chance to change your mind, dude. When I'm done with you, you will never be the same person again."

"Dude, fuck you. I don't care about that anymore."

"That is pretty obvious," he breathed before plunging in deep, driving his cock forward until he was hitting my prostate. I bit my bottom lip as I tried not to scream. The feeling of having him penetrating me like this involved a lot of pain, but also a lot of pleasure.

I had never felt like this before in my life.

When Carl was fully inside of me, he stopped what he was doing before making a question, "How are you feeling? Do you want me to go slow?"

I nodded. There was no point in hurrying things over.

I couldn't see his face, but I knew that he was smiling. He started to roll his hips as he pounded in and out of me. Moments later, he picked up his pace before his stick started to throb.

And I came at the same time with him, losing my consciousness soon after. I knew that I was becoming his bitch and it was the best thing that could've happened between us.

I was never going to forget this.

The End

Check out the first book of the series here (or just go to the next page for a sneak peek):

1. Caught Looking by the Quarterback

Lastly, leave a review if you liked the book. It always helps me so much!

SNEAK PEEK: CAUGHT LOOKING BY THE QUARTERBACK

Straight to Gay First Time Story (Bicurious Guys - 1)

I was just a college guy, like all the others. I was trying to fit in and look less like an idiot. Why did I have to stumble into the college's football team, though? I didn't know, but things were working out this way. More and more girls were beginning to show interest in me, even if it was only momentary… and I didn't think it was going to lead anywhere.

I sighed, closing the door by my side when I realized someone was there. Not too far from me, taking off his shirt and getting ready to put on his uniform. I supposed it was appreciation more than anything that was making me feel this way about the guy, even though I was 100% straight. Really, I was, and nothing was going to change that.

But nothing could have gotten me ready for what I was seeing. The guy was perfect. He was in his early twenties, so he was a little older than me, huge, with rippling muscles, and a beard still to be made. His hair was jet-black and his eyes the color of emerald. Every time he looked at me, he froze me with his gaze.

I couldn't stop thinking about him, even when he was in his room and wasn't doing anything more than playing on his computer. I wasn't going to say I was gay. I really wasn't, but I couldn't stop admiring him for being everything I wanted to become. Perhaps he could help me with working out at the gym, but then I didn't know if I'd be able to hide my boner… like it was happening now.

Not only I wasn't gay, but I also had to keep reminding myself that I wasn't a virgin, either. Not in the usual, more common sense of the word, at least. I had some experiences where it kind of happened with some girls… And I'd like to keep things at that.

Austin was now taking off his pants too, and I couldn't stop dissecting his perfect legs with my eyes. I couldn't help but imagine what it would be like to slide my hands over his muscles, feeling his hair, the curves that defined his legs, and smelling the scent of his crotch. Why was I thinking about those things of my team's leader?

I didn't know, but I was already feeling desperate and my boner was beginning to show. I came here with a common pair of jeans and it should be enough to keep it hidden. Austin could never find out that I had a huge turn-on for him, or else there would be trouble. This was a small college in the middle of nowhere, in a region known for being pretty homophobic. I didn't want to take the risk and then be forced to transfer to another university. It wasn't going to happen.

I took a deep breath and looked away quickly when he turned slightly. I didn't know if he was looking at me or not. We were in the dresser room and everything was pretty quiet here. Everything was so silent I could almost hear a pin dropping. I was a couple of feet away from Austin and I was pretty sure he wasn't thinking anything odd was happening here. After all, he had no reason to believe I was gay.

I took a deep breath in, looked back where he was, and I realized he was back to putting on his uniform. But he was still taking off his socks this time. He wasn't looking as imperious as before because he was seated now, his back turned to me.

But it wasn't that seeing him that way was making him look any less lust-inducing than he was. Even now, my body was frozen and I hadn't made much progress in terms of putting on my uniform. I needed to do that when my cock wasn't so hard. I should be punching myself that I was feeling those things for the guy that was always so willing to help everyone out, but it was just… impossible to control my feelings.

I heard the door opening and I knew that meant that things here were going to get more complicated. I could hear them talking out loud, cracking jokes, and laughing. It was the rest of the team. They were walking into the dressing room and were going to see that I was stealing glances at the quarterback…

BICURIOUS SERIES
AND MORE

EXECUTIVE SUBMISSION

1.Hard in the Office 1: A Straight to Gay MM Story

2. Hard in the Office 2: No Pity for the Miserable Incel

3. Hard in the Office 3: An Incel's Tale of Degrading Humiliation

4. Hard in the Office 4: Bending the Incel Boss

5. Hard in the Office 5: Taming the Incel Spy

6. Hard in the Office 6: Lectured by the Boss

OBEY ME

1. Prep School Obedience 1: A Straight to Gay MM Story

2. Prep School Obedience 2: Phil is Punished

3. Prep School Obedience 3: Phil is Lectured

ABOUT THE AUTHOR

Michael Levi's biggest passion? Writing steamy, romantic stories that leave his readers panting. He's currently focusing on Omegaverse steamy romances, but his collection is diverse and there are books for everyone's tastes. If you're looking for straight to gay, first time, BBC, ABDL, and more, you're going to find them on his author page.

He lives to pamper his readers, every kiss means a lot more than what meets the eye, and he loves his Alpha males. Making sure that every gay first time feels different, Michael Levi writes his stories with a cup of coffee by his side. And for inspiration, he always opens a photo of his new crush.